WHATCHA GO

by Jennifer Dussling
illustrated by Amy Wummer

The Kane Press
New York

For Kelsey—J. D.

Text copyright © 2004 by Jennifer Dussling. Illustrations copyright © 2004 by Amy Wummer.

Library of Congress Cataloging-in-Publication Data

Dussling, Jennifer.
  Whatcha got? / by Jennifer Dussling ; illustrated by Amy Wummer.
    p. cm. — (Social Studies connects)
  "Economics - grades: 1-3."
  Summary: When Megan learns that *Very Vintage*, her favorite television show is coming to her hometown, she decides to search her house for antiques to take to the show.
  ISBN 1-57565-143-2 (pbk. : alk. paper)
  [1. Collectors and collecting—Fiction. 2. Antiques—Fiction. 3. Television programs—Fiction.] I. Wummer, Amy, ill. II. Title. III. Series.
  PZ7.D943Wh 2004
  [Fic]—dc22
                                                2003024181

10 9 8 7 6 5 4 3 2 1

First published in the United States of America in 2004 by The Kane Press.
Printed in Hong Kong.

Social Studies Connects is a trademark of The Kane Press.

Book Design/Art Direction: Edward Miller

www.kanepress.com

The monetary values for objects mentioned in sidebars on pages 6, 9, and 16 were researched on the following websites:
www.coinsite.com
www.postalmuseum.si.edu
www.collectbooks.about.com
The addresses and content of websites referred to above are subject to change.

I ran into the living room, grabbed the remote, and turned on the TV. Just in time I heard those magic words. "Whatcha got?"

It was *Very Vintage*, my favorite TV show ever!

Long ago, a person who was hard of hearing used an ear trumpet, like this one.

Very Vintage went to a different city every week. People brought in old stuff—and the experts on the show told them what it was worth.

The best one of all was Justin Justelle. He was a real pro. He always knew what everything was worth. I'd never seen him stumped.

Vintage is a fancy word for old. Some old things are called **antiques**. There is no strict rule about how old an antique has to be— some experts say 100 years old or older.

My little brother, Baxter, liked *Very Vintage*, too. He sat next to me with his teddy bear. We watched the experts look at some silver dishes, a glass lamp, and an old tool called a sugar cutter. Justin said that hundreds of years ago sugar came in a loaf, so you needed something to cut pieces from it. Who knew?

This is worth about $200!

Why are some old things worth a lot, while other old things are just—old? One reason is **scarcity**—when there is not enough of something. If something is **scarce**, and a lot of people want it, it's worth a lot more!

Then a lady showed up with a small wooden box. Justin lifted the lid. Inside were some old coins, shiny and gold. The lady had found them while she was digging in her garden.

I held my breath. Justin told her what they were worth. *Woo-hoo!* Two thousand dollars!

That's why I like this show so much. Real people find real treasures all around them.

Scarce, or rare, coins are worth a lot to coin collectors. A 1932 gold Indian Head Eagle coin is worth about $280, but one dated 1933 (just one year later) is worth over $40,000! Why? Not many were made that year.

The rest of the hour flew by. Music came on, and a man's voice said, "*Very Vintage* is on the road again. We're headed for St. Louis, Cleveland, Cincinnati, and Gradyville."

I blinked twice. Did he say *Gradyville*? Gradyville is where I live! *Very Vintage* was coming to my town! I let out a whoop. Then I ran to tell my mom the good news.

"Can we go, Mom, can we, huh?" I begged.

"Okay, Megan," she said.

Now all I needed was a treasure that would make Justin Justelle jump for joy—and get *me* on TV!

"Do we have any swords?" I asked. Old swords are usually worth lots of money.

"Swords?" My mother almost choked on the word. "Not in this house, young lady!"

"Stamps printed upside down?" I tried.

"No," she said.

In 1918, the post office made a mistake when it printed two million airmail stamps. On a few, the airplane was printed upside down! Only 100 are known to exist. Those 24¢ stamps are now worth almost $200,000 each!

I sighed. "What about diamond necklaces?"

My mom smiled. "Nope. No diamond necklaces, either."

"Letters from dead presidents?" I asked hopefully.

"No, Megan." She laughed.

I didn't know why Mom did that. What was so funny?

Old letters signed by famous people can be very valuable. So can printed things like old baseball cards, magazines, posters, newspapers . . .

I looked around. We had to have something valuable somewhere. "Everything is too new!" I groaned.

"Try the basement," Mom said. "There are some old boxes down there from Grammy's house. We never unpacked them."

Finally, Mom was being helpful.

Baxter and I went downstairs. The boxes were in a corner covered with dust. That was good. It meant they were old. Vintage!

Either that, or Mom wasn't a good housekeeper.

Some newer things can be worth a lot, too, because people collect them. A *Star Wars* Darth Vader action figure cost a couple of dollars in 1977. Today it is worth hundreds of dollars! That's because lots of people collect *Star Wars* figures.

The first box was full of dishes. Once I saw
a *Very Vintage* show where a hand-painted plate
from France was worth seven hundred dollars.
This box could be a gold mine!

I pulled one out. It was yellow with orange
ducks. It looked hand-painted. The ducks were
kind of blurry, like when a painting gets smeared.

Yay! My first big find. I put it in my bag.

I opened another box. It was filled with photographs. Photographs could be worth good money. The best ones were black and white and had a famous person in them.

The top picture was black and white. Maybe this guy was famous!

I put the picture in the bag, too.

Another box had old shoes in it. I'd never seen old shoes on the *Very Vintage* show. But you never know.

I put them in, too.

Sometimes old clothing can be valuable, even old shoes. Remember the ruby slippers from *The Wizard of Oz*? They're in the Smithsonian museum in Washington D.C.!

In the rest of the boxes I found a telephone, some old books, a cup with a moose head for a handle, a hooked rug, and a glass statue missing one arm.

Baxter went through the boxes, too. He put four pens and an ice cream scoop in with my stuff.

Some people collect rare books. The first edition of a book—one of the books from the very first printing—is usually the most valuable. The first edition of *Harry Potter and the Philosopher's Stone* (printed in England in 1998) is worth about $10,000—and its value goes up every year!

The last box was the best of all. It had a painting in it! Justin Justelle almost always got excited over paintings.

This one was a beauty. It was a sunset over an ocean. There was no name on it, but I bet it was done by somebody famous.

I hauled the bag of stuff up the stairs. Baxter came, too.

"Mom! Mom!" I yelled. "You were right. Grammy had great stuff. Very vintage," I said. I laughed at my own joke.

The three days until Saturday went verrrry
slowwwwly.

Finally, it was the big day. Mom drove us to
the high school. That's where they were having
Very Vintage. We followed the signs to the gym.
We walked through the big doors, and then—I
was there!

Huge signs hung from the ceiling. Tables were set up along the edges of the gym. Everywhere I looked, people were standing in long lines.

It was so cool!

21

Mom took us to one of the lines. We stood there and waited. And waited. I counted the people in front of me. Twenty-three.

We waited some more.

Baxter lay down on the floor. He rested his head on his teddy bear and looked at the ceiling.

We waited, and waited, and waited. Now and then I heard a squeal. That was someone with a treasure!

FINALLY, we made it to the front of the line. And there he was. "Hi, Mr. Justelle!" I squeaked.

He gave me a dazzling smile. "Hi, little collector!" he said. "Whatcha got?"

I felt a tingle in my neck when I heard those famous words. I couldn't speak. So I dumped my stuff on the table, instead.

VERY VINTAGE

Justin's mouth made a big "O." He was amazed at the stunning beauty of my many treasures! Or maybe he was just stunned by how many there were. There *were* an awful lot.

Justin picked up the painted plate. "Hmm," he said. "It's from Macy's, circa 1982."

Now, 1982 was a long time ago, but most *Very Vintage* things are much older. I didn't think that was a good sign.

"Fifty cents," he told me.

One by one, he went through all of my things. Nothing was worth more than a dollar—not even the painting.

Fifty cents!

One dollar!

"Circa 1982" is a fancy way of saying "from around 1982."

Justin started to call for the next person in line, when something caught his eye. "Wait!" he cried. "What's that?"

The camera swung my way. I had a treasure after all! I smiled my biggest smile.

But the camera wasn't pointing at me. It was pointing at Baxter!

Justin snatched Baxter's teddy bear from him. He held the crummy old bear like it was gold, or diamonds, or an old sword.

He looked at the bear's paw. "*Aaaaaaah*," he said softly. "Yes. A Stiffenbach Bear."

The camera came in closer. "Do you know what this is worth?" Justin asked my brother.

Baxter shrugged.

"Only one hundred of these were made eighty years ago," said Justin. "So, even as . . . er . . . well-loved as it is, this bear is worth a thousand dollars."

"A thousand dollars?" I gasped. "Wow!"

"Where did you get it?" asked Justin.

My mom answered for Baxter. "It was mine when I was little," she said. "And my father's before me."

"Well-loved" is a nice way of saying "worn." Usually, collectors like things that look as good as they did when they were new.

"It's a true treasure," Justin said. He handed the bear to Baxter. Baxter hugged it tight.

I could tell he didn't care what it was worth. Baxter would love that bear if it were worth fifty cents. And maybe that's what a real treasure is.

Three weeks later, we watched *Very Vintage* from Gradyville.

There was Baxter and his teddy bear on TV. And if you looked closely, you could just see ME!

hmmm

Baxter's grandpa probably never guessed that his teddy bear would be worth a lot one day. What do you have that people of the future might want? Hmmm . . .

scarcity
and value!

MAKING CONNECTIONS

Scarcity is when there is not enough of something to go around. Just about anything can become scarce—especially things that lots of people like to collect, such as baseball cards. Jackie Robinson was the first African American to play major-league baseball. Collectors will pay a lot for signed Jackie Robinson baseball cards because they are scarce and many people want them.

Look Back

Justin Justelle uses what he knows about the scarcity of certain objects to estimate their value. Look at page 9. How many upside-down stamps were printed? Why are they worth so much money? What does Justin say about Baxter's teddy bear on page 29? What makes these bears so valuable?

Try This!

When is one penny worth more than one cent? When it is scarce! Did you know that 100 years ago people used pennies with a picture of an Indian on the front? Today, these "Indian Head" pennies can be worth a lot to coin collectors.

Start your own collection! What are you interested in? Would you like to collect coins, stamps, buttons, trading cards, comic books? Keep notes about each object you collect and why it's special. For lots more information on collecting, visit the Smithsonian website: http://kids.si.edu/